E   Herman, Gail
HERMAN,
GAIL

Lowl
jo
Circ

$10,34

DATE DUE

Lowly Worm
Joins the Circus

The Recycling Plant

Busytown Airport

12
The Flour Mill

11

10

8

7

9

Stadium

April
Rhino's
House

The Port

1. HUCKLE'S HOUSE
2. HILDA'S HOUSE
3. SGT. MURPHY'S

4. PIG FAMILY HOUSE
5. MR FRUMBLE'S HOUSE
6. FIRE STATION

Welcome to Busytown!

t Busy
ervatory

Ski chalet

Camping Grounds

Busy Bay Point

Bruno's Snack Stand

The Beach

Busytown Grand Hotel

The Train Station

Sea Fort

SIMON SPOTLIGHT
An imprint of Simon & Schuster Children's Publishing Division
1230 Avenue of the Americas
New York, New York 10020
Copyright © 1998 by the Estate of Richard Scarry

First Simon Spotlight edition, 1998.

Designed and produced by Les Livres du Dragon d'Or
All rights reserved including the right of reproduction
in whole or in part in any form.
Adapted from the animated television series *The Busy World of Richard Scarry*,
produced by Paramount Pictures Corporation and Cinar.

READY-TO-READ, SIMON SPOTLIGHT, and colophon
are registered trademarks of Simon & Schuster.

Manufactured in Italy
10 9 8 7 6 5 4 3 2 1

Library of Congress Cataloging-in-Publication Data
Scarry, Richard.
Lowly Worm joins the circus. — 1st Simon Spotlight ed.
p. cm. — (The busy world of Richard Scarry) (Ready-to-read. Level 2)
"Adapted from the animated television series: The busy world of Richard Scarry"—Copr. p.
Summary: Lowly Worm discovers that being a circus performer is not as wonderful as he
thought it would be—especially if it means giving up your family.
ISBN 0-689-81625-1 (pbk.)
[1. Circus—Fiction. 2. Animals—Fiction.] I. Title. II. Series.
III. Series: Ready to Read. Level 2.
PZ7.S327Ly   1998
[E]—dc21   97-39941
CIP   AC

Lowly Worm
Joins the Circus

Adapted by Gail Herman

Ready-To-Read

Simon Spotlight

Hooray!
The circus has come to Busytown!

Everyone rushes to the big circus tent.
"Welcome to my circus!"
announces Top-Hat Fox.
"You will see incredible feats!"

"Behold the Flying Bearlendas!"
Top-Hat Fox says.
"They are the best trapeze artists
in the world!"

"Yay!" shouts the Cat family.
They sit in the very first row.

"I wish I could do that," says Sally.
"Me too!" Huckle adds.
"I *can* do that!" Lowly says proudly.

All too soon,
the show is over.
"Thank you for coming," says Top-Hat Fox
as everyone leaves the tent.

"Did you like
the circus?"
Mother Cat
asks Lowly.
"You bet!" he says.
"I would love to be
in the circus myself."
Lowly springs high in the air.
Look! Someone else is watching Lowly!
"Hmm," whispers Top-Hat Fox to himself.

Back at home,
Huckle and Lowly put on their own show.
"Welcome to Huckle Cat's Family Circus!"
Huckle announces.
"And now here's Lowly,
the Wonder Worm!"

Lowly flips and flops
and tumbles head
over heel.

Just then,
Top-Hat Fox
drives by.
He sees Lowly's
acrobatics.
"Wow!" says
Top-Hat Fox.
"There he is again!"

The Cat family cheers for Lowly.
"Bravo!" exclaims Mother Cat.

"That was great!" Father Cat says.
"No," says Top-Hat Fox.
"That was *extraordinary!*"

Top-Hat Fox shakes Lowly's foot.
"We would have to change your name,"
Top-Hat Fox says to Lowly.
"But how would you like
to join the circus?"
Lowly's eyes open wide.
"Would I ever!"
he says.

"That is a big decision,"
Father Cat says.
Huckle jumps up and down.
"He *has* to do it, Dad!" says Huckle.
Top-Hat Fox grins.
"Come," he tells Lowly.
"Let's meet your new family."

"Hey!" says Huckle.
"*We're* Lowly's family."
But Lowly doesn't hear.
He is walking away
with Top-Hat Fox.

Top-Hat Fox shows
Lowly around the circus.
"Here is the strongest rhino on earth!"
says Top-Hat Fox.
"Ugh!" grunts Strongo the Rhino.

"And this is Miss Puss,"
Top-Hat Fox says.
"She can bend into *any* shape!"

Soon it is showtime!
Lowly takes a deep breath.
"Here I come!" he says,
as he hops into the tent.

Top-Hat Fox bows to the audience.
"And now," he announces,
"the one . . . the only . . .
LOUIE Worm!"

The Cat family is again
sitting in the first row.
"Does Lowly really have a new family?"
asks Sally.
"We'll always be Lowly's family,"
Huckle says.

Lowly juggles four bowling pins.

Then he twists around and catches them.

"Oooh!" the crowd shouts.

When the show is over,
everyone crowds around Lowly.
"Louie, Louie!" they scream.
"Can I have your autograph?"
"Me too!"
"Please!"

"Lowly," Huckle calls out.
"Lowly!"
Finally Huckle shouts,
"Hey, Louie, it's me!"
Lowly pokes up his head.
"Hi, Huckle," he replies.
"Do you want my autograph?"

Just then,
a clown yells
to Lowly.

"It's time to celebrate your first show,"
the clown says.

Huckle watches Lowly
walk away with the clown.
"I don't want your autograph,"
Huckle says sadly.
"I just want you to come home."

Backstage, everyone is packing up.
"Our show is over,"
explains Top-Hat Fox.
"We'll be in Pleasantville tomorrow."
Lowly gulps.
"But how will I get home
to my family?"
he asks.
"*We're* your new
family, Louie,"
Top-Hat Fox
replies.
"And the circus is
your new home."

Lowly feels terrible.
He looks at a picture of Huckle, Sally,
and Mother and Father Cat.
"I don't want a new family
or a new home!"
he says.

The Cat family is upset too.
"Why did they call him Louie?"
asks Sally.
"That's a stage name, dear,"
Father Cat replies.
"Lowly is a circus star now."

Suddenly,
Lowly hops through
the window!

Plop! He lands
in his chair.

"Lowly!" everyone exclaims.
The Cat family gathers around
and hugs Lowly tight.
"It was fun to be a circus star,"
Lowly says.
"But it's so much better
to be a star
right in your own home!"

New words to know:

Announces

Incredible

Feats

Family

Whispers

Acrobatics

Extraordinary

Decision

Strongest

Showtime

Audience

Juggles

Twists

Autograph

Celebrate

Backstage

Terrible

Exclaims

Gathers